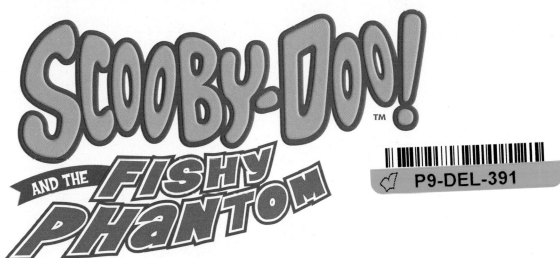

SCOOBY-DOO!
AND THE FISHY PHANTOM

By Jesse Leon McCann

P9-DEL-391

SCHOLASTIC INC.

New York   Toronto   London   Auckland   Sydney
Mexico City   New Delhi   Hong Kong   Buenos Aires

Dedicated to my son, Jesse Blake, talented cartoonist and forever my pride and joy

—J.L.M.

No part of this publication may be reproduced, stored in a retrieval system, or transmitted in any form or by any means, electronic, mechanical, photocopying, recording, or otherwise, without written permission of the publisher. For information regarding permission, write to Scholastic Inc., Attention: Permissions Department, 557 Broadway, New York, NY 10012.

ISBN-13: 978-0-439-78807-6
ISBN-10: 0-439-78807-2

Copyright © 2006 Hanna-Barbera. SCOOBY-DOO and all related characters and elements are trademarks of and © Hanna-Barbera. (s06)

Published by Scholastic Inc. All rights reserved. SCHOLASTIC and associated logos are trademarks and/or registered trademarks of Scholastic Inc.

20 19 18 17 16   15 16/0

Printed in the U.S.A.   40

First printing, April 2006

Designed by Michael Massen

Special Thanks to Dan Davis for cover and interior illustrations.

Scooby-Doo and Mystery, Inc. arrived at the Coolsville Aquarium for a private after-hours tour. Velma had just won first place in the Science Fair, and the tour was the prize!

Everyone was excited. They would be the first visitors to see the aquarium's newest attraction, the beautiful and rare rainbow flounder!

"Hello! Hello!" Mr. Winterbottom, the aquarium's head curator, greeted them.

"Jinkies! Listen to this," Velma exclaimed. "'The Coolsville Aquarium is home to more than 12,500 ocean animals!'"

"That's correct!" Mr. Winterbottom said proudly. "But, before we start the tour, let's stop by our underwater snack bar so we can get some dinner!"

"Like, great idea!" Shaggy gulped.

Scooby nodded in agreement.

Steve Curly, the snack bar manager, wasn't happy about staying open late. He muttered angrily, but the gang didn't hear him. They were too preoccupied looking around at their impressive surroundings— the snack bar was sixteen feet under water!

"Let's go see our rainbow flounder, shall we?" asked Mr. Winterbottom.

On the way to the rainbow flounder exhibit, Mr. Winterbottom became upset with a janitor who was slowly mopping the floor in the same spot. "Why are you still here?" the curator scolded. "You are the slowest janitor I've ever seen!" The gang felt sorry for the old man.

It was at the rainbow flounder's tank that they got a bigger surprise than they could have imagined! Someone was stealing the priceless fish!

"I am the Fishy Phantom," cackled the intruder. "And the rainbow flounder is mine!"

"Help! Help!" Mr. Winterbottom cried, as the Fishy Phantom fled the scene.

"Don't worry, Mr. Winterbottom, it won't get away," Fred said. "Go check with security to make sure that all the exits are secured. Daphne, Velma, and I will follow the Fishy Phantom," Fred continued. "Shaggy and Scooby, you go the other direction. We might be able to box it in! Come on, gang—we've got another mystery on our hands!"

"Like, let's check the snack bar first," Shaggy suggested. "Maybe that freaky fish is hungry!"

"Reah!" Scooby agreed. They were both hoping to get some more snacks.

"*Raaaargh!*" the Fishy Phantom roared. "I told you to leave me alone! Now you're in for it!"

"Zoinks! We were only looking for snacks, Mr. Fishy!" Shaggy pleaded.

"Ruh-huh! Racks!" Scooby agreed.

"SNACKS?" growled the Fishy Phantom. "Now you're going to be *my* fish food!"

The creature chased Shaggy and Scooby through hallways and tunnels, over catwalks, and up and down escalators.

Then Scooby-Doo got an idea. He and Shaggy grabbed some scuba gear and jumped into a fish tank.

"Like, great plan, Scoob!" Shaggy talked loudly, so he could be heard underwater. "That creepy crawdaddy will never find us in here!"

"Ree hee hee! Reah!" Scooby-Doo laughed. "Reepy rawdaddy!"

"*Raaaargh!*" The Fishy Phantom was suddenly rushing toward them as fast as a torpedo!

"Zoinks! Swim for it, Scoob!" Shaggy cried. "He's back, and he brought friends!"

Shaggy swam as fast as he could, making long strokes with his lanky arms and quick kicks with his fins. Scooby-Doo dog-paddled with all his might!

Meanwhile, Daphne, Velma, and Fred made a *very* interesting discovery. The old janitor was sneaking around. He seemed a lot more energetic than before.

"He's up to something," Daphne whispered. "I just know it."

"He's acting awfully suspicious," Velma agreed.

"Come on," Fred said. "Let's check him out."

"Hold it right there!" Fred shouted.

"Wh-what are you doing in here?" the janitor cried. "I-I'm just finishing up for the night!"

Daphne and Velma spotted the glow of rainbow colors behind the old man. "It's looks like you've got some explaining to do," Velma said to him.

"You've caught me," the man said. "I'm not really a janitor, I'm—"

"Cal Cooley, from the Coolsville Action News squad!" Velma interrupted. "I've seen your exposés on TV. They're nothing but sensationalized gossip!"

"This view screen was making the rainbow glow!" Daphne reported. Cooley had gone undercover as a janitor to get footage of the rainbow flounder for his news show!

"Shame on you, Mr. Cooley," Velma said as they escorted the reporter out. "You knew the aquarium wanted to keep the rainbow flounder's image a secret!"

Just then, Shaggy and Scooby showed up. When they saw that the TV reporter was leaving the aquarium, they wanted to leave, too.

"Oh, no you don't," Daphne said. "We haven't solved this mystery—yet."

"Listen, gang, I've got a plan to capture this Fishy Phantom," Fred explained. "And we have all the things we need to set a trap, right here in the aquarium."

"Like, does that include Scoob and me as bait?" Shaggy asked, frowning.

Fred admitted that it did. At first, Scooby and Shaggy refused to do it, but when Velma tempted them with a box of Scooby Snacks, they agreed to help.

A few minutes later, the trap was set and everyone was in place.

"Like, I hope Fred's plan works!" Shaggy said. "I'd hate to think I dressed up this silly for nothing."

Scooby looked at Shaggy and started giggling. Shaggy *did* look pretty funny!

"What are you giggling at, man?" Shaggy asked. "You look just as ridiculous!"

The Fishy Phantom couldn't believe it! Shaggy and Scooby were in the big tank, laughing! Not only were they not hiding in fear, it looked like they had stolen the rainbow flounder from the spot where it was stashed!

"ARRGH!" the Fishy Phantom howled angrily, as it jumped into the tank and swam swiftly in their direction.

The Fishy Phantom approached the net. Fred was ready to tug on the rope to bring up the net, but something went wrong! The net didn't catch the Phantom at all! Shaggy and Scooby were forced to flee from the monster again!

Outside the tank, Fred and the girls were puzzled. "Jinkies!" Velma exclaimed. "I think something else tugged on the rope!"

Minutes later, the creature had cornered Shaggy and Scooby inside the dark and deserted gift shop.

"*Hrrm!*" growled the Fishy Phantom. "Give me what's inside that goldfish bowl!"

"Zoinks! Whatever you say, man!" Shaggy cried.

The light from the camera was so bright that the Phantom couldn't see a thing!

"*Yaaaaaaah!*" the Fishy Phantom yelled.

The rest of the gang followed the creature's scream to locate Shaggy and Scooby.

"Jeepers! It's Steve Curly, the snack bar manager!" Daphne exclaimed, after Fred removed the Fishy Phantom's mask.

"Like, wow!" Shaggy scowled, as Scooby sniffed indignantly. "To think we let you cook us dinner!"

"Steve Curly hid the rainbow flounder in his pantry so he could sneak it out after hours and sell it!" Velma explained.

"I would have gotten away with it, too, if it weren't for you meddling kids!" growled the manager.

"Now the rainbow flounder is safely back in its tank," said Mr. Winterbottom happily. "Let's go take a look!"

The Mystery, Inc. gang was amazed by the beauty of the rainbow flounder!

"Thank you, kids!" the curator said. "The rainbow flounder is now safe for everyone to enjoy!"

"This mystery wouldn't have gone so swimmingly without our Scooby," Velma smiled.

"Scooby-dooby-doo!" cheered Scooby-Doo.